## YOUR HOT STORY
## HAS JUST TURNED
## EXPLOSIVE!

"There's just one question I'd like to ask you," you tell LaPelle.

"Okay, if you promise only one."

"I understand your brakes were sabotaged last week. Does this mean that someone has it in for you?"

LaPelle bolts upright and looks at you angrily. "Certainly not! Why would anyone want to hurt me?"

Just then there's a sudden crash of glass behind you. An object skitters across the floor and under the table—sticks of dynamite, and the fuse is burning! You jump back, the smell of burning cordite filling your lungs.

You start to reach under the table, your impulse telling you to grab the bomb and toss it out the window. But perhaps you should run for the door and hope to get out in time.

Seconds are ticking away. What will you do?

## ONLY *YOU* CAN DECIDE . . .

D1103811

A CHOOSE YOUR OWN ADVENTURE® BOOK

# PASSPORT

## TOUR DE FRANCE

### Book 1

### By James Becket

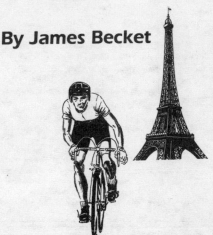

### Illustrated by Howard Simpson

### An R.A. Montgomery Book

BANTAM BOOKS
NEW YORK • TORONTO • LONDON • SYDNEY • AUCKLAND

RL 4, age 10 and up

TOUR DE FRANCE
A Bantam Book / April 1992

CHOOSE YOUR OWN ADVENTURE® is a registered trademark
of Bantam Books,
a division of Bantam Doubleday Dell Publishing Group, Inc.
Registered in U.S. Patent and Trademark Office and elsewhere.

Original conception of Edward Packard
Cover art by Aleta Jenks
Interior illustrations by Howard Simpson

ISBN 0-553-29443-1

Published simultaneously in the United States and Canada

Bantam Books are published by Bantam Books, a division of Bantam
Doubleday Dell Publishing Group, Inc. Its trademark, consisting of the
words "Bantam Books" and the portrayal of a rooster, is Registered in
U.S. Patent and Trademark Office and in other countries. Marca Reg-
istrada. Bantam Books, 666 Fifth Avenue, New York, New York 10103.

PRINTED IN THE UNITED STATES OF AMERICA

OPM    0  9  8  7  6  5  4

*To my daughters, Daphne and Sandra*

## Welcome to the WCYA Passport News Team

**Y**ou are a special correspondent for the WCYA Passport news team. A few years ago you were the winner of a local contest for a children's television announcer. You were teamed with Edwina—known as Eddy—who is a writer, and Jake, a cameraman. You quickly became the hottest news team in the business. Now the three of you travel the world on assignment, always looking for the next scoop.

Your current assignment is to cover the Tour de France, the most famous bicycle race of all time. You're there to cover the story, but in the process you uncover some very serious wrongdoings.

In the pages that follow, you will be asked to make a choice from time to time. You could expose some kidnappers and be cited for your bravery. Or your reporting could get you into trouble: enemies may want to kill the story—and you!

Good Luck!

"**M**urder? That's a pretty serious charge, Eddy," you say, looking out the hotel window at the Eiffel Tower.

It is a beautiful July day. You and your cameraman, Jake, have just arrived in Paris to cover the Tour de France, the greatest bicycle race in the world. At the moment you'd just like to sleep, but your colleague Edwina, known as "Eddy," insists that you could be covering more than a bike race in your report. In one of the preliminary heats, France's top racer and national hero, Marcel LaPelle, has met with a minor accident.

"I'm convinced someone tried to kill Marcel LaPelle," Eddy replies. "It was not an accident. I was there. I saw the cuts in the brake."

"What did the police say?" you ask.

"That's just it," Eddy answers. "LaPelle and his trainer seemed extremely upset, scared even, that I'd seen the brakes. They insisted it was an accident. That's what made me suspect something."

Jake sits up on the bed. He's an amateur bike racer and really knows the sport. "Eddy, come on," he says. "The Tour de France is like a religious event here. Wars would stop just to have the Tour. No one would dare hurt LaPelle, let alone try to kill him."

→ → → → → → → → → → → → →

*Go on to the next page.*

# 2

Eddy turns. "Jake, get real. The Tour today is also big business. The riders are cycling billboards. Companies put up millions to get their name in front of the public. Towns compete to get the Tour to pass through their streets. With so much fame and money at stake, you can't tell me no one might be tempted to have an 'accident' happen."

You realize they are both right. The Tour is a great sports event, probably the toughest athletic test around. Riders face a twenty-five-hundred-mile endurance race over twenty-five days through flatlands and valleys and up and down mountain roads steep enough to make goats think twice.

The course varies each year, but always finishes in Paris with the riders sprinting up the Champs Elysées to the Arc de Triomphe. One year it goes clockwise around France, the next counterclockwise. The race is run in daily stages, with the winner of the previous day's stage wearing the *maillot jaune*, or yellow jersey, and starting at the head of the pack the next day.

At the same time, the Tour de France is a huge commercial event. More than twenty million passionate fans wait for fleeting glimpses of their favorites as they flash by in their brilliant red, yellow, green, blue, and violet jerseys—tires humming on the pavement accompanied by the snick-snack of changing gears.

→ → → → → → → → → → → → →

*Turn to page 36.*

Jake fastens a thin, transparent wire on the bike's frame right below your handlebars. Eddy guns the motorcycle. The wire goes taut, and suddenly you feel yourself being pulled along. What a relief! Now you can pedal faster, with no resistance. It's so easy.

The pack comes into view ahead. Jake gets out his camera and makes like he's filming you. You start to pass riders on the outside. You keep your head down and pump furiously. Now you thank the fog and the rain, for making the wire even more invisible. As you pass them, the riders look up. Some shout, "Who is this rider?" You're covered with mud thrown up from the bikes' wheels—you could be almost anyone.

You leave the pack behind in the fog. The road now climbs steeply, but your motorcycle escort makes the run a breeze for you. Up ahead you see the lone yellow jersey.

O'Steen pays no attention to Jake as he passes, but when you pull alongside, he nearly falls off his bike with surprise. He pumps harder. Eddy speeds up and you stay close to O'Steen, pumping fast.

"Hey," O'Steen says between labored breaths, "I'll make a deal. We take turns in the lead, I'll let you win the stage today."

→ → → → → → → → → → → →

*Go on to the next page.*

Riders are always making deals like this. Working together, rather than fighting each other, they can take turns leading and breaking the wind for each other, thus helping both their performances. O'Steen wants to win the Tour; one day's stage is not that important for him.

"Okay," you agree, "if you answer a few questions."

He nods.

"Who's behind Team X?"

"Hey, under my contract I can't say anything. Besides, I don't know."

"I think whoever it is kidnapped LaPelle."

O'Steen looks worried. "LaPelle is conceited. He deserved to fall, but not to be kidnapped. I wanted to beat him fairly."

"Do you have any idea?"

You're nearing the top of the pass. "Last night we were in Geneva, and I saw my trainer with a man who . . . "

O'Steen's bike suddenly skids off the road, his front wheel gone flat. He curses and leaps off. Normally a teammate would give him his wheel, as O'Steen is the one with the chance to win. You stop pedaling to get off your bike, forgetting you're in tow. Eddy and Jake are looking ahead. You brake, but you're still being pulled, and your locked wheel skids on the wet road. Fortunately O'Steen is so preoccupied he doesn't see what's happening.

Finally Jake looks around and quickly cuts the wire. You manage to keep your balance, turn back, and come alongside a desperate O'Steen. You get off and start to remove your wheel for him.

"Who was the man in Geneva?" you ask O'Steen.

The blue and yellow car of his trainer roars out of the fog. The doors open and the trainer, a tough-looking man, is out immediately with a wheel. An assistant trainer also leaps out. He takes your bike and helps replace your own wheel. You look at O'Steen, hoping for an answer. But you see immediately that he won't talk with his trainer there.

O'Steen leaps on his bike and pumps the few yards to the top of the pass. You get back on your bike and ride after him. At the top, you can see into Switzerland. A rainbow spans the verdant Rhône Valley as the storm clears. The road drops sharply down in front of you in a series of tight switchbacks.

You have to decide fast. Should you try to catch up to O'Steen? If you can, he might tell you the name of the man. The course is all downhill, but you could be risking your life on the steep, wet road. You could always wait and try to talk to him later. Jake is shouting behind you.

→ → → → → → → → → → → → →

*If you decide to go after O'Steen,*
*turn to page 39.*

*If you decide to play it safe,*
*turn to page 42.*

The policeman at the reception desk of the *commissariat de police* bursts out laughing. "Not another one! Every year it's the same—we get twenty stories like this. Bring me a body, then we can talk." He notices your total frustration, shrugs, and hands you a sheaf of papers. "Here, fill these out. I will submit them to my superiors."

Eddy and Jake are waiting expectantly on the street. They see from your expression that you struck out.

"Grab your equipment, I'm not giving up," you growl. After all, you're a professional journalist. Getting doors slammed in your face comes with the territory.

You enter a side door. The police officer on duty notes your impressive-looking camera and sound equipment. You flash him your press card. "We're here to interview the *commissaire* about his investigation of the attempt on Marcel LaPelle's life."

"*Un moment, s'il vous plaît,*" he says politely as he reaches for the phone.

To your surprise, five minutes later you find yourself facing the *commissaire de police* in his high-ceilinged office. You relate what you know, and his face gets redder and redder. You begin to feel foolish. Not only is he unconvinced, the more you talk, the less you believe the story yourself.

→ → → → → → → → → → → → →
*Go on to the next page.*

The *commissaire* raises his hand to stop you. "We are anxious to have good relations with the press. However, when journalists, especially vulgar sports journalists, attempt to create a scandal from nothing to sell their papers, that is not acceptable!" He rises from the chair. "Get out of my office and stick to covering sports, not fantasy!"

You, Jake, and Eddy drive out of Paris a pretty glum trio. You've missed the start of the Tour in Versailles, with nothing to show for it. You decide to concentrate on doing some first-class sports reporting when you catch up with the Tour at Calais.

In midafternoon you pull off the road at a bistro recommended in your guidebook. Eddy reads the menu: the two specialties are frog legs and snails. When you ask the waiter if they serve French fries, he tells you he's never heard of them.

You are surprised to see such a crowd in the bistro at this hour. Farmers, shopkeepers, the postman, and all the locals are in for a glass of wine. You see why when a sudden cheer goes up around you. They're watching the Tour on television.

The finish of the first day is on the screen, live from Calais. LaPelle and O'Steen are neck and neck heading toward the finish line, with Oswald Hinckley, a teammate of O'Steen's, close behind. Each man pumps his pedals with his last ounce of strength. LaPelle drives through to win over O'Steen, who is nipped at the finish by his teammate Hinckley. The bistro erupts in a roar of cheering.

You interview some of the livelier characters, trying to get a sense of why the Tour is so popular. Many have ridden to the bistro on their bikes, dressed in the cycling outfits of their favorite teams. They argue with great passion about their favorites.

You catch up to the Tour on the second day as the riders swing south and move along the coast of the old duchy of Normandy, named after the conquering Northmen—the Vikings—who settled in France in the ninth century.

Over the next few days you work hard reporting on the sights and the race. You're so caught up in the excitement, you've all but forgotten about the possibility of murder. Marcel LaPelle certainly isn't riding like a man scared to win. After six days he's wearing the *maillot jaune*, signifying his status as leader of the race.

→ → → → → → → → → → → → →

*Go on to the next page.*

# 12

The next few days take you and the riders through the Loire Valley, a fertile region studded with *châteaux*, or castles. On day eight, the riders will head through Bordeaux, the area of southwestern France famous for its fine red wines.

On the ninth day you hire a helicopter to get some aerial shots. As Jake hangs out precariously with his camera, you take in the great view—the red tile roofs of the villages, the plush green fields, the endless rows of grapevines, the rolling hills. Directly below you, the two hundred riders look like a speckled serpent wiggling its way along a ribbon of highway.

Someone breaks from the pack! It's the yellow jersey—LaPelle. He appears to be taking a gamble. The Pyrenees are near, and it is there and in the Alps, the two great hill-climbing parts of the race, that many say the race is won or lost. If LaPelle wins a big enough lead before the mountains, he could have a near lock on the title; if he exhausts himself and falls back, he could be throwing the race away.

→ → → → → → → → → → → → →

*Turn to page 14.*

# 14

LaPelle is now well out of sight of the others, but from up above you can see it all, both the pack and the lone rider in the yellow jersey. And yours is not the only helicopter following the race. A black, French-made Alouette has been on your right for the last ten minutes.

You look down as the pack approaches a blind corner. A haywagon is approaching from a side road. From above, you can see an accident about to happen. As the wagon crosses the road, the riders come around the corner doing about thirty miles per hour. The first cyclists swerve to avoid the obstacle. Two go down, and like dominoes, the rest of the pack knock each other down or career off into the bumpy fields. It's a total catastrophe. And what a break for LaPelle to be out of harm's way!

You search ahead for the familiar yellow jersey. You can't believe your eyes. The black helicopter has landed, and two men appear to be dragging LaPelle toward it. His bicycle is overturned on the road. "What's happening?" Jake blurts out.

The black helicopter rises quickly. "There's only one explanation," you say slowly. "LaPelle is being kidnapped!"

Your pilot hovers over the crash site. Some riders have gotten back on their bikes and gone on, but a number just lie there. They could be seriously injured. Men standing over the fallen riders are waving wildly at you for help. The other helicopter banks off toward the west, its prisoner aboard. Should you chase it to try to save LaPelle? Or should you land and transport the seriously injured to the nearest hospital?

→ → → → → → → → → → → → →

*If you decide to help the injured, turn to page 30.*

*If you decide to chase LaPelle's kidnappers, turn to page 16.*

# 16

The helicopter trembles and shakes as your pilot opens full throttle in pursuit of the kidnappers.

"Jake, did you get that?" you shout over the roar of the engine.

Jake pats his camera and gives you the thumbs-up. No one is better under fire. The tape might help identify the kidnappers. Already you're imagining sending a copy to the *commissaire* in Paris who threw you out of his office.

A sharp ping resounds above your head. The pilot curses violently in French at a figure in the black helicopter, who is firing a rifle at you! Your chopper veers off to the right, as your pilot fiddles with the radio dial.

"They knocked out our radio," he reports. "We cannot now radio our position to alert the air force. What do you want to do?"

"What do you suggest?" you ask him.

Your pilot, a Frenchman and avid cycling fan, regards ruining the Tour as the most terrible of crimes. "Follow them. We can stay back out of range, and follow them on the radar if we lose sight of them."

You turn to Jake and Eddy. They nod in agreement. They want to go for it. No one else will prevent the kidnappers from making a clean getaway.

For more than an hour you trail them, often losing visual contact in the billowing white clouds. The helicopter shakes violently with the turbulence of updrafts. You're flying dangerously close to the Pyrenees, through narrow gaps in the peaks. Through the mist, you see what looks like an avalanche but turns out to be a large flock of sheep, frightened by the noise of the helicopter. You can see the shepherd, no doubt a Basque, and his dogs working to contain them.

The pilot of the Alouette does his acrobatic best to shake you off. Your pilot tries to keep up, but your radar only works when there's no mountain between you and your quarry. You swoop over a ridge. Down below looms a large town.

The pilot looks surprised. "That's Andorra. We've come further than I thought."

Andorra is a postage-stamp-size country, half the size of New York City, wedged in the mountains between Spain and France. Its inhabitants have become prosperous with tourism and—some say—smuggling.

Where is the black helicopter now? There's no blip on the radar and nothing in your line of vision. Have they landed or flown off in some unknown direction?

→ → → → → → → → → → → → →

*Turn to page 19.*

"Down there!" Eddy shouts.

The clouds below you part for a moment, revealing a huddle of stone buildings on the mountainside. You don't see any helicopter. A flash of movement in a courtyard catches your eye. It's the rotor blades of the black chopper winding down. The cloud bank rolls through below, swallowing up the buildings.

The pilot nods. "I saw it. It looks like an old monastery down there, isolated in the mountains."

What should you do? You have no radio to alert help and send your position. If you go back for help, LaPelle might be gone by the time you return.

Part of the reason you've gotten ahead so fast in your profession is your ability to make lightning decisions, more often than not the right ones.

"Jake, you and Eddy go back with the pilot," you instruct. "Get the police right away, then file the story to the station. We've got an exclusive on the most daring kidnapping of the century right on tape!"

You point out the window to a small plateau on the mountainside just above the cloud-shrouded monastery. "Leave me there, so I can keep an eye on the kidnappers. We don't want to lose them before the police arrive."

→ → → → → → → → → → → → →

*Go on to the next page.*

# 20

Eddy and Jake stare at each other. They're obviously scared for you, but they see you're determined.

The helicopter hovers above the stony ground, and you climb down a rope ladder, jumping the last feet and rolling to absorb the shock of the fall.

As the helicopter ascends out of the mountains, you realize how alone you are. Help should be on its way soon, though.

But then the helicopter abruptly jerks in the sky. A thin trail of smoke darts from its tail. It quickly loses altitude and plummets behind a mountain. *Oh no*, you think. They must have taken a hit from a gun at the monastery. You can only pray your friends survive the crash. But even if they do, there's no way word of where you are will get to the authorities.

You move to the edge of the rock shelf you're on and look down toward the monastery. You quickly spot at least a dozen men with guns climbing toward you. Only one way to go. Up! You run across the ledge and start climbing higher through scrubby trees. The sound of barking dogs comes from behind you.

You come to a new chain-link fence and climb up and over it, your vaulting skills enhanced by sheer fear. Soon you're off the monastery grounds.

You keep climbing. It's steeper and steeper. You pull yourself hand over hand up a small cliff.

Go on to the next page.

You lift yourself up to a ledge and stare face-to-face at—a lion! What's a lion doing in the middle of Europe? And what are you doing hanging off a cliff looking at one? Change the channel, you think. You back down a few steps and look below. Is that a tree trunk or a giraffe's neck? It's a giraffe. What is going on? You see now the place is teeming with animals. You must be in some kind of game park. The fence was to keep the animals in.

Zing! A bullet whizzes past you and ricochets off the rock above your head. You look down. Your pursuers are not far behind.

You make it to the top of the mountain. At first glance it seems like a flat plateau, but then you see there's a natural bowl, like an ancient theater. At the bottom of the cup are scores of large birds: eagles, condors, vultures, hawks. The men are getting closer, and you realize there's no escape.

→ → → → → → → → → → → → →
*Go on to the next page.*

# 22

You rush down the slope of the bowl, setting off a cascade of stones and sending the birds into a frenzy. Their legs, you notice, are tied by cords to stakes in the ground.

A man appears above on the rim of the bowl, then another. You are totally surrounded. You have to do something. What about gathering up the cords from several birds? They are eager to escape, and you are light. Maybe, just maybe, they could lift you out.

Then again, trying such a risky escape might not be wise. Why not just show the men your press card? Kidnappers have to make demands, and the press can be useful in delivering messages.

A dozen men start down the slope of the bowl. You must decide now.

→ → → → → → → → → → → → →

*If you decide to fly out with the birds,
turn to page 24.*

*If you decide to show your press card,
turn to page 93.*

**Y**ou perch at the edge of the window. "It's at least fifteen feet down!" Jake cries.

"Jump!" you shout. You leap into the night air. You land hard, but you're okay.

Jake thumps down next to you, and you both sprint down the sidewalk to your van, jump in, and drive off.

You arrive at Mr. Kako's walled-off estate. You check the camera, pointing it at Jake. His image appears on the van monitor, which means the camera's working.

"This is one big risk," Jake says. "First you have to transmit to me, then I send the signal to the local station, they uplink it to a satellite, WCYA picks it up, and then it's rebroadcast to the world. Those are a lot of links that can go wrong. Have you checked your batteries?"

But you're already out the door heading for the gate.

You ring the bell. Loud barking erupts from the far side of the wall. Through the grill, a huge house looms in the darkness like a castle. Footsteps approach. The gate opens. You immediately recognize the big man behind it as the one talking on the portable phone to Kako when Hinckley died.

The man leads you past a swimming pool. The water is churning with movement under the surface. Maybe it's just a big Jacuzzi.

→ → → → → → → → → → → → →

*Turn to page 95.*

Hurriedly you yank up a number of stakes, wrapping the birds' cords around your waist and arms. The birds, sensing freedom, go berserk, flapping their wings and colliding with one another. Up on the rim, your pursuers can only watch the whir of flapping wings and flying feathers in amazement.

You wonder desperately how many birds it will take to get you off the ground. You're glad you skipped a heavy French lunch.

You feel your feet leave the ground. The birds flap their wings, mightily straining for the sky, and you rise right out of the bowl.

You're now a hundred feet above the plateau. The birds head out over the valley. The men below have gathered their wits and are wildly shooting at you.

You thought you were scared down there in the bowl, but at least you were on solid ground. Now you must be two thousand feet above the valley floor. You feel dizzy. The circulation in your arms is being cut off by the cords. You want so much to let go. Not only that, your shirt is full of feathers, and they're tickling you unbearably.

Each bird seems to have its own idea of where it wants to go, but each time they try to fly off in different directions, you all plummet down a few hundred feet. Your stomach feels as if you're in a high-speed elevator.

You can only wonder where you're going to end up. Maybe in an eagle's nest high up on a pinnacle of rock, a place you'll never get down from.

You feel one of the cords around your arm unwind. Then it comes loose! A giant condor soars upward, flying free. You begin to lose altitude. There's your answer about how to get down—release just the right number of birds. But it has to be the right number, or you'll crash. You unwind one more cord, and a hawk flies off.

# 26

You start to descend quickly, and the ground rushes toward you. You just hope one of your birds doesn't spot a mouse and decide to dive-bomb it.

The birds are flapping exhaustedly as you descend toward a field. You feel you're going too fast to land safely. You see a pile of hay and one of manure. Both would break your fall, but you definitely have a preference. You pull on the cords, and the birds respond. You're only twenty feet above the haystack. The birds stop flapping and spread their wings to land. You fall straight into the hay. You've made it!

→ → → → → → → → → → → → →

*Turn to page 28.*

You undo all the cords, letting the blood flow through your arms again. The grateful birds take off. You look back up the mountain. There's no way your pursuers are going to catch up with you in the next few hours.

You spot a car coming down a nearby road and run across the field to flag it down. It's a blue station wagon. You're in luck—it's the French *gendarmerie*. At your desperate waving, the policemen stop.

"Please, we've got to act fast. There are some men with guns after me and some birds flew me out and dropped me here . . . " You stop talking as you realize you sound as if you've escaped from an insane asylum. Fortunately, the police don't understand English. It's time to talk with your hands and body.

"LaPelle, Marcel LaPelle." That they understand. You point to yourself. "Journalist." Then you point to the mountain, "Helicopter, LaPelle, prisoner." The *gendarme* understands and reaches in to grab his radio mike.

Based on your information, the police move in quickly and surround the kidnappers. A police helicopter rescues Jake, Eddy, and the pilot who were forced down. You're there for every minute of it, getting the exclusive story. When the kidnappers surrender, Jake appears with his camera in time for you to interview Marcel LaPelle. All LaPelle can talk about is how grateful he is to you for saving his life.

LaPelle is rushed back to the Tour, which had been suspended. At the press conference, there are more questions for you than LaPelle. Your only difficulty lies in trying to explain how you got down the mountain so fast. If only Jake had been there with the camera to film the birds!

LaPelle goes on to win the Tour, and you have a place of honor at the award banquet in Paris. The next morning you fly back to WCYA studios.

The outer office drops to a hush when you arrive. One of the secretaries says, "Mr. Peterson wants to see you. He's really angry."

How could that be? You step into his office. Peterson snarls from behind his desk, "So there you are, back at last. I thought you were a journalist. I send you out there to cover a story, and what happens—you *become* the story! I see your face on every newspaper and every TV screen. What's going on?"

He looks stern. You gulp. Maybe you've violated some journalistic ethic you didn't know about.

Then Mr. Peterson bursts out laughing, comes out from behind his desk, and gives you a bear hug. "Congratulations! That's the most amazing piece of work I've seen in my thirty-two years in the business. I knew you were hot, but not sizzling. Just tell me one thing—how did you get down from that mountain so fast?"

**The End**

You signal your helicopter pilot to land. He nods and sets the craft down quickly by the side of the road, the wash of the big blades blowing up papers and dust.

Two Tour medics are already at work on the most seriously injured. As you help lift one man with a spinal injury into the helicopter, the medic tells you, "He'll have a fighting chance now. By road he wouldn't have made it."

You rush to the local television station and send off your story by satellite. You are the only

ones who have footage of the actual kidnapping. It's a real journalistic coup.

You sit in a small editing room, rerunning the tape over and over, looking for clues to the kidnappers' identity. The helicopter has no markings, and even through Jake's zoom lens, the features of the men remain indistinct.

→ → → → → → → → → → → →

*Go on to the next page.*

The evening news reports that the kidnappers have disappeared into thin air. There has been no ransom demand. The news also reports that Tour officials have decided to suspend the race for a day.

The day passes, and there is still no word from the kidnappers. The Tour resumes. "Poor LaPelle," Jake says to you and Eddy.

"I'm sure he has bigger concerns than the race right now," you comment. "But I don't know what else we can do except keep covering the Tour. Maybe we'll turn up some clues."

"If anyone stands to gain from the kidnapping, it's Shaun O'Steen and Team X," Eddy says. "Let's talk to them."

You try to talk to Shaun O'Steen, but he refuses all interviews. After each day's finish he is whisked off to seclusion by his trainer. The press is angry, regarding these tactics as a publicity strategy to increase Team X's mystery.

As the Tour moves across the south of France, through Provence, and turns up toward Grenoble and the Alps, you try every trick you can to get to O'Steen. You have no success. Four days after the kidnapping, there is still no word about LaPelle. Now the Tour has taken second place in the public eye to l'affaire LaPelle. The newspapers are full of reports that he has been spotted in Bangkok or Argentina and speculation that this is all a government plot to take people's minds off economic problems. If the police have any clues, they're not sharing them with the press.

As the Tour reaches the Alps, the crucial point of the race, you grow discouraged by your failure to interview O'Steen. Then Jake comes up with an idea. "The only time we ever see O'Steen is when he's out racing, right? Why don't you join the race, ride alongside him, and talk to him? He'll be making his big attack in the Alps, so he'll be out in front all alone."

You shake your head. "Come on, Jake, he's one of the best in the world. Uphill in those high altitudes, I couldn't keep up with him for a hundred yards, much less hold a conversation."

Jake just smiles. "Trust me. I have a plan for Chamonix."

Chamonix, a town which bills itself as the mountain climbing capital of the world, is host to thousands of climbers each summer who come to enjoy the sport of *alpinisme* and test themselves against some of the most challenging rock walls in the world. The majestic Mont Blanc, Europe's highest mountain, rises above the valley at 4,807 meters, or 15,771 feet.

→ → → → → → → → → → → → →

*Go on to the next page.*

# 34

At noon on the day the Tour goes through the Chamonix Valley and over the *Col des Montets*, you are standing on the side of the road with Jake and Eddy. You're at the far end of the valley, where the road starts to climb toward the *col*, or pass.

Not only can you not see the mountains, you can hardly make out your hand in front of your face. It is pouring rain, and there is a thick fog. Under your rain poncho you are dressed in a complete cycling outfit. Your gloved hands grasp the handlebars of a sleek, lightweight racing bicycle. You're feeling pretty miserable, but Jake says the fog is perfect, it will allow you to blend in much better and not be caught by the race officials.

"They're coming," Jake shouts, as you hear the sound of motors down the road in the fog.

Since the road is closed to traffic for the Tour, the approaching din must be the caravan of trainers, officials, and the media. You mount your bike. The first cars come by. You're hoping O'Steen is alone in the lead, so you can ride alongside him. Your heart pounds. You hear the riders before you see them, some four hundred slender bike wheels hissing on the wet road. Jake pushes you, running alongside to give you a good start. The pack appears out of the fog, and you pedal madly, trying to locate a comfortable gear. The rain comes down in sheets, and you're soaked in a matter of seconds.

You settle in at the edge of the pack. Your adrenaline pumps from nervousness and exertion. You get in a rhythm, and it starts to feel good. You look around. The riders seem quite relaxed, almost casual. They're just cruising along. Many are eating sandwiches. A few look over at you, but now that you're soaked, you probably look as if you belong. They're all waiting for some biker to make a break for the lead, when the pace will really pick up. Where is the yellow jersey? Up ahead you see O'Steen. How will you ever work your way up through the pack to get next to him, much less talk to him?

O'Steen breaks into a sprint and goes out in front. The pack is suddenly electrified. The riders bear down, pedaling faster. You pump hard to keep up, gasping for air, your lungs burning. The road angles upward. In the heavy fog, you've already lost sight of O'Steen. You slip back, unable to keep up. In a minute you're all alone.

You hear a motorcycle behind you. It's a BMW with a sidecar, and leaning out is a smiling Jake. Eddy is the driver.

"Now for phase two of the plan," Jake shouts. You'd love to chew him out, but you're so out of breath you can't talk.

← ← ← ← ← ← ← ← ← ← ←

*Turn to page 4.*

Racers pedaling across the loveliest countryside in the world are followed by an endless caravan of Tour sponsor vehicles, their flashing billboards stuffed with paper hats and plastic bags to be thrown to scrambling fans on the roadside.

Hundreds of millions more will watch the riders on TV or catch photos of the day's winner on the front pages of local newspapers. The country comes to a standstill for the race. To ride in it is an honor, to finish a remarkable achievement. To win it is absolute glory.

With so much pressure and competition, temptations to take shortcuts certainly exist—but murder?

On the flight over, you read up on this year's race. Marcel LaPelle is aiming for his fourth straight victory. He's one of the most popular but also one of the most controversial riders in history. LaPelle's long-time rival, Shaun O'Steen, ranks as a cofavorite. His team, Team X, is new, and poses a real mystery. The riders dress in black, with no insignia at all. According to the team trainer, a wealthy philanthropist backs the team to defend the purity of the sport and make a statement against commercialism. Cynics call it an advertising ploy, to keep everyone guessing what X is. When the world's curiosity is at a fever pitch, the owners will reveal the product and sell millions. But whoever is backing Team X has put together the toughest group of riders on the Tour, the true "bad boys" of a sport known for its dangerous high-speed falls and collisions.

You, Jake, and Eddy have prepared for the grueling marathon as best you can. Fortunately you have just received your driver's license. Cameras, recorders, an ice chest, even a laptop computer sit in a rented van that Eddy has had equipped with a microwave dish to allow you to connect with nearby TV stations.

For the last eight months, you, Jake, and Eddy have been on "open assignment" for WCYA, a top network news channel. Instead of making you coanchor with the veteran newscaster, who threatened to quit if you shared the hour, Derek Peterson—the president of the channel—has sent the three of you on the lookout for special shows anywhere in the world! It's an unbelievable break. You remember Mr. Peterson's words: "You three are hot! Get out there and show your stuff. No holds barred."

Jake and Eddy are very excited about covering the Tour de France. While you love sports, you felt the assignment was a bit tame. Now that Eddy has come up with a whole new spin on the race, you're ready to get in gear.

→ → → → → → → → → → → → →

*Go on to the next page.*

# 38

The race starts tomorrow in Versailles, outside Paris, then moves north to Calais, continuing counterclockwise around France—south and west along the beaches of Normandy, down the Atlantic coast, and through the wine country around Bordeaux to the Pyrenees.

After the Pyrenees, it's north and east across Mediterranean France, and through Provence, a land of warmth, olives and vines. From there the riders proceed to the towering Alps, where the Tour dips into French-speaking Switzerland before heading west, then north through Burgundy to finish in a blaze of glory in Paris.

Can Marcel LaPelle survive the trek if someone is indeed after him? You, a journalist, have a story to investigate.

"So where do we start?" you ask.

"I think we should go to the French police investigators, the *Sûreté*," Jake proposes. "If something did happen to LaPelle, it would be a disaster for France. The police might already know about it, and we could break the story."

Eddy smiles. "We could do that, but what about talking to LaPelle directly? We could ask for an interview."

The race is set to start in a matter of hours. Time is short.

← ← ← ← ← ← ← ← ← ← ←
*If you decide to go to the Sûreté, turn to page 9.*
→ → → → → → → → → → → →
*If you decide to interview LaPelle,
turn to page 63.*

You push off, pedal once, and your bike picks up speed down the steep incline almost as though you were in free-fall. The first turn is banked. You lean into it. You catch sight of O'Steen no more than a hundred yards ahead. You hunch over the handlebars to cut down your wind resistance.

You're gaining on O'Steen. You must be doing at least fifty miles an hour. Up ahead you can see the first switchback, and beyond that the valley. O'Steen suddenly seems to be coming back. You're catching him! You must be doing close to seventy now. O'Steen's braking. You squeeze your brakes on the handlebars. You don't slow at all!

You look down. The wire to your brakes is cut! You shoot by O'Steen. You sit up straight, trying to cut your speed with wind resistance. The corner comes at you so fast that you have no time even to think of leaning into it.

→ → → → → → → → → → → → →
*Go on to the next page.*

# 40

You zoom straight between two stone guardrails and fly off into space. You and your bicycle seem to hang for a moment out in the void. Then you plummet. Two thousand feet below is the peaceful meadow of a Swiss farm. Setting a record for the fastest descent of the *Col des Montets* in the Tour de France is not what you thought the last achievement of your life would be.

## The End

You stare down the steep road. Trusting the sinking feeling of total fear in your stomach, you stop and turn as Jake runs up to you.

"Don't go!" he says, trying to catch his breath. "I'm sure he cut your brakes. I've got it all on tape."

You look down, and sure enough, the wire to your rubber wheel brakes has been cut. Team X's assistant trainer must have done it while "helping" you put your wheel back on.

"Now we've got real proof—let's go to the police," Jake says with growing anger.

You look up. The trainer and his assistant are getting back into their blue and yellow car. "Hold on," you tell Jake. "We want to find out about LaPelle. Cutting my brakes doesn't prove anything on that score. It just shows they're scoundrels."

The pack appears, laboring mightily for the summit. The riders sense they're at the end of the day's agony of effort. Once over the top they'll cool off, then face the fear of racing down a mountain where the slightest mistake could kill them.

When the pack has passed, you look for the blue and yellow car. It's headed back toward Chamonix. "That's strange," Eddy comments. "It should be following the race."

"Follow them!" you say. You leap behind Eddy, and the three of you start back down the mountain.

You, Jake, and Eddy follow O'Steen's trainer's car to Chamonix. They drive straight through the town without stopping, and at the head of the valley turn toward Geneva, Switzerland.

The day has turned sunny, with great, white, billowy clouds. The glacier-covered mountains and pine-forested slopes are spectacular. You zip along, never losing sight of the Team X car, hoping they don't realize you're following them.

You pass through the French town of Annemasse and come to the Swiss border. The blue-uniformed French customs officers wave you past, as does the stern-looking, gray-coated Swiss. You're in the outskirts of Geneva, and you are immediately struck by how different it is from France. Everything is neat and prosperous-looking.

Geneva is located at the end of a long lake the residents call Lake Geneva. The Rhône River goes through Geneva on its way to the Mediterranean. The city is a famed international center, hosting the European headquarters of the United Nations and scores of international humanitarian agencies, such as the International Red Cross. It's also known for its watches, chocolate, and banks. Switzerland has long been a neutral country, a safe haven for refugees and money. As you follow the Team X car into the center of town, you wonder if LaPelle is being held prisoner right here in Geneva.

→ → → → → → → → → → → → →

*Turn to page 45.*

The Team X car slows and stops in front of an impressive-looking bank on the Rue du Rhône. The trainer jumps out and strides into the building.

You, Jake, and Eddy step inside the marble-floored bank just in time to see the trainer disappear into an elevator. There's no way the guard will ever allow you on that elevator. You busy yourselves reading brochures on how to manage your fortune.

Ten minutes later, the elevator door opens and the trainer steps out. He shakes the hand of a man with an eye patch, whom Eddy immediately recognizes. "He's Poli Kako, the electronics magnate," she whispers. Mr. Kako shakes hands with two somber men sporting long, thick beards, one of whom is carrying a large briefcase.

You step outside into the street, just as the four men come out, behaving as though they don't know each other. Kako turns right, while the two men walk left toward the Pont du Mont Blanc, a bridge that crosses the Rhône. The trainer waits for a moment and then follows Kako. You're sure the men's actions have something to do with the kidnapping. You just have to make the right decision. Whom should you follow?

→ → → → → → → → → → → → →

*If you decide to follow Kako, turn to page 84.*

*If you decide to follow the two bearded men, turn to page 51.*

You decide to stay at the tour and examine the videotapes of the incident. You and Jake sit bleary-eyed at the editing console, watching the bank of TV monitors. You've already sent off your story for the day, but you want to search closely for any clues about Hinckley's death.

"Go back to that part where the official takes off LaPelle's jersey," you say. Jake runs the tape backward and stops. "You see that limousine in the background, the window coming down? Is there any way you can zoom in on that?"

"Sure." Jake pushes various buttons, and you get a blowup shot of one part of the screen. A man with an eye patch is talking into a telephone. He's shouting and seems very upset.

Suddenly you remember something. "Jake, put up the tape from French TV, the part right before Hinckley went down."

→ → → → → → → → → → → → →

*Go on to the next page.*

# 48

An image of the top of the hill and the spectators appears on the monitor. You shout, "There!" and point to a large man talking on a portable cellular phone. "Put up the man in the limousine on the other monitor!" You're very excited now. Both tapes have a time code in a little box at the corner that gives the exact time the image was shot. "See, the time is the same—they're having a conversation. I wish we had a shot from the other side. We're onto something, Jake, but we need help."

→ → → → → → → → → → → → →

*Turn to page 86.*

"Those men you saw me with in the bank were Corsican Mafia," Poli Kako says. You remember that Corsica is a windswept island in the Mediterranean, Napoleon's birthplace. "They kidnapped LaPelle, and they want five million dollars for his release. I said I would pay two million, and they accepted it. I wanted to save a man's life, of course, but also I have an interest in the Tour de France. I turned over the ransom money to them. Now we must be patient and await LaPelle's release."

Kako sees you to the door. "Remember, you promised not to write anything until LaPelle is safe."

You nod. You, Jake, and Eddy are driven to your hotel by a chauffeur, where you order a *chocolat chaud*, good Swiss hot chocolate. Eddy says, "How do we know that he wasn't paying off those guys for doing the kidnapping?"

"We don't," you reply. "But we have to wait a while. I wouldn't want to jeopardize LaPelle's chances for survival."

Two days later, LaPelle is found a few blocks from his house in Marseilles, wandering in the street. He remembers nothing about the kidnapping. Doctors determine that he was drugged, but otherwise he is in good shape.

→ → → → → → → → → → → → →

*Go on to the next page.*

You go to Paris to cover the final day of the Tour, which Shaun O'Steen and Team X win. You break the story that Kako Electronics is behind Team X. Mr. Kako is on hand to share the glory, and to announce that LaPelle will be joining Team X, now Team Kako, next season.

Rumors abound about what happened to LaPelle, but the truth remains a mystery. You don't have any evidence other than Kako's word that the Corsican Mafia were behind the affair. WCYA calls you back to Boston for a new assignment. You leave France with a bittersweet feeling, wondering whether you could have gotten the true story if you'd done things differently.

## The End

You follow the two bearded men, who are striding toward the Pont du Mont Blanc. You cross the bridge behind them. Jake and Eddy follow you on the motorcycle.

The two men head up the Rue du Mont Blanc toward the railway station, the Gare de Cornavin. Eddy gets in line behind them, and watches as they buy tickets for Perpignan, a city near the Pyrenees and Spanish border. She purchases three tickets, and you all hurry to board the train. In a few minutes you are in a comfortable compartment, heading once again toward southern France.

Fifteen hours later you dismount at Perpignan. The two men are met by another bearded man in an old car. You follow them in a taxi through mountain hamlets and into Basque country, a land of chalet-shaped houses with red beams crisscrossing whitewashed walls and sloping roofs of bright red tiles.

→ → → → → → → → → → → → →
*Go on to the next page.*

The origins of the Basque people, you have read, are a complete mystery. They are no relation to the French or Spanish and their language has some possible kinship only to Finnish and Hungarian. Perhaps the kidnapping has something to do with the Basque nationalist movement which seeks independence for the area from Spain and France.

You ascend a narrow dirt road high into the mountains. The taxi driver informs you that the road leads to an old monastery that has been taken over by a religious sect. "No one knows anything about them," he says. "They keep to themselves."

Coming around a corner, the taxi is suddenly face-to-face with a closed gate. You can tell by the dust in the air that the old car has just gone up the road on the other side. "We'll have to continue on foot," you say.

"Be careful," the driver warns. "Those people are very strange. I've heard they believe another Great Flood will come to cover the earth, to punish man for his arrogance in destroying the planet."

Three hours later you're still hiking up the steep, forested mountainside toward the monastery. The closer you get, the more alert to danger you are. Eddy, in the lead, holds up her hand. You stop and listen. "I'm sure I just heard an elephant trumpeting," you say.

Turn to page 55.

# 53

Eddy shakes her head and you listen harder. A snoring comes from behind a tree. As you skirt quietly around it, you see a man's leg. It's a roly-poly, bearded monk, sound asleep. You smile at Jake and Eddy with relief, until you see the sub-machine gun next to the monk.

Tiptoeing past him, you climb quickly higher. Seeing the gun has made you more certain that you may be close to LaPelle. You hear something up ahead. A cacophony of animal sounds competes with loud banging and sawing noises.

→ → → → → → → → → → → → →

turn to page 55.

You step out on a ledge. Below is a totally unbelievable sight: an enormous wooden boat, at least 300 feet long and 150 feet wide. Men, women, and children are working on deck, hammering, sawing, and painting. Near the boat are vast pens full of animals—zebras, gazelles, aardvarks, giraffes, elephants, and more. You remember the taxi driver's words. These people, like Noah with his ark, must truly believe another Great Flood is coming.

You, Jake, and Eddy look at each other in total amazement.

"This must be what they need money for," Eddy says. "A project like this has to cost millions."

Jake suddenly slaps a mosquito feeding on his arm.

"Jake! How could you do that?" you tease. "These people have gone to such trouble to get two of every species. You've just killed half their mosquitoes."

Remembering what you came for, you whisper, "Come on, let's check out the monastery for LaPelle."

You hurry single file over the pine-needle carpet of the forest. Shafts of sunlight pierce through the canopy of trees above. You come to a clearing containing a large clothesline weighted with monks' robes and camouflage combat fatigues. You each grab a robe.

You go through more woods and finally see the gray slate roof of the monastery ahead. Nearby you hear voices approaching. A ladder leans against the wall of the building. You motion the others to follow as you begin to climb.

You scramble up the slippery slate roof and hide behind a chimney. From this vantage point you have a clear view of the cloister below and the entire monastery complex.

A double wooden door opens—and LaPelle is led out by a group of bearded men. Even though he's blindfolded, you're sure it's him. He's taken through an archway outside the monastery. His captors return to the cloister, leaving their prisoner with a single guard. Behind you, several boat workers head through toward the cloister. It looks as if they're getting ready for some kind of meeting.

A group of children arrive on bicycles near LaPelle. They leave their bikes and enter the cloister.

You glance at your two friends. LaPelle's life seems to hang in the balance. He must be rescued fast. Eddy speaks first. "I think we should go for help right away."

"I don't know if there's enough time," you answer. "But one of us *should* go. Eddy, why don't you? Then I can go down and try to get LaPelle on one of those bikes and no one will catch him."

"It looks too risky to go down there with all those people around. I have another idea," Jake says.

"Well, what is it?" you ask.

Jake smiles. "Just trust me, I guarantee it'll work."

This habit of Jake's drives you nuts. It's too much like gambling. You want to know exactly what your options are, not to play games.

Down below the meeting looks ready to start. You have to decide.

Eddy starts down the roof. "I'll leave you two to decide what to do. I'm going for help."

→ → → → → → → → → → → → →

*If you want to take your chances on Jake's plan,*
*turn to page 71.*

*If you want to sneak down to rescue LaPelle,*
*turn to page 61.*

"Run for it!" you cry. You and Marcel LaPelle dash madly for the door. As you burst outside, you turn to shout to Jake and Eddy to hit the dirt. But before a word leaves your mouth, you get clobbered by a bicycle. Your leg buckles, and you collapse. Then a heavy ladder falls on top of you.

You've collided with a chimney sweep, pedaling along carrying his ladder. He seems to be all right as he gets up and brushes dirt off his black outfit. You know you're hurt pretty badly.

At a nearby hospital, X rays confirm that you have a broken arm and leg. Jake tells you the bomb that made you run for your life was only a joke.

You spend the next three weeks in traction with a series of ropes, pulleys, and weights keeping you and your cast motionless. You watch the Tour on TV. LaPelle comes in second. His efforts end up only helping Shaun O'Steen to win. You feel that there was something going on, but you're not the one who's going to find out. You use this time to do research on your next assignment. The Tour for you has been a total bust.

## The End

When you get back, you are heroes. You give Jake full credit for the idea, and Eddy credit for having the police waiting at the bottom of the mountain.

LaPelle decides the bicycle ride down the mountain has been his last. He announces his retirement from racing and rushes off to join his wife and daughter.

When the leaders of the sect are questioned by the police, they confess they were paid by Kako to kidnap LaPelle. They needed money to finish their boat. Since they believed they were saving the human species, they felt justified in disobeying any human laws.

Kako denies it all, saying that he paid the ransom as a humanitarian and patriotic gesture. But later, at the trial, the evidence is clear that Kako orchestrated the kidnapping in a desperate attempt to save his bankrupt industrial empire. He is sentenced to twenty years in jail.

Your only regret is that no one got to film the stampede. There will never be another like it, unless of course someone makes a movie of your adventure. You have in fact received a number of offers from Hollywood, in addition to a reward from the French government. You, Jake, and Eddy decide to donate the money to the World Wildlife Fund to find homes for all the animals. After all, they saved your lives.

**The End**

You decide to rescue LaPelle while you have the chance. After climbing off the roof, you and Jake saunter casually around the corner of the monastery. LaPelle squats on the ground. His guard is watching the meeting inside. When LaPelle rubs his shoulder against the blindfold, you realize he can see a little.

You manage to mount one of the bicycles despite your heavy robe. Holding the handlebars of another bicycle with your free hand, you start pedaling toward LaPelle. Jake approaches the guard, whom he plans to do his best to distract if the man turns around. But your foot suddenly won't move on the pedal. Oh no! Your robe is caught in the chain. You keel over with a crash.

The next thing you know, you wake up in a stone dungeon. LaPelle and Jake stare down at you. Jake's face is bruised.

Just then you hear footsteps outside. The dungeon door creaks open. Someone is thrown into the dark cell with you. It's Eddy!

A hulking man stands in the doorway. "Now nobody knows you're here. But it will make no difference, because everyone except us will soon drown. It is foretold that the rains will begin today. It will rain for forty days and forty nights. The rain will melt the ice cap. The oceans will rise, and all the land will be covered on the fortieth day." He slams the door behind him.

→  →  →  →  →  →  →  →  →  →  →  →  →

*Go on to the next page.*

Through the window opening you can just see a little patch of gray light. It is pouring outside. Water rushes through a drainpipe onto the floor of your cell. In only a few minutes it's above your ankles.

At least when you die, it won't be of thirst.

## The End

You telephone Marcel LaPelle for an interview, but your efforts to reach him fail. The one time you get through, someone tells you curtly that *"Le Champion"* is not giving interviews. He is in seclusion, preparing himself for tomorrow's start. At least you know where he'll be later—the town of Versailles, where the Tour will begin.

As you drive your rented van into Versailles, you are halted by a dense mob of Parisians and cycling fans. You can't get anywhere near the town square, where the Tour is to start.

You stop a minute to gaze at the gray-stoned palace, built by Louis XIV and finished in 1682. You try to imagine one king and his family living in such a huge "house", with its endless pillars and arches and the acres and acres of formal gardens out front. You recall that the palace was sacked during the 1789 French Revolution by a mob of Parisians. King Louis XVI and his wife, Marie Antoinette, were later beheaded by the guillotine.

→ → → → → → → → → → → →
*Go on to the next page.*

The police help you make your way through
the crowds toward the press area. The race is
about to start. The town square is full of flowers
and the air electric with anticipation. The ath-
letes warm up in a roped-off area and make last-
minute checks of their bicycles. You spot Marcel
LaPelle, sitting upright, balancing on his sleek
racing bike just a few yards from the start. He
wears the yellow jersey from his victory last
year. He is a tall man, with long legs, and you see
how his proud carriage and aquiline nose have
earned him the nickname *"L'Aigle,"* or "The Eagle."

There's no way you can get through to him now, and this is hardly the moment to ask him if someone is trying to kill him. You'll see soon enough on the road if he's a man afraid to win. You and Jake work on getting the camera in a good position for the start.

The 220 riders bunch together as the count-down begins. For this Tour there are twenty-two teams, each with 10 riders. The race is very much a team effort, with each team supporting its lead rider, the man with the best chance to win.

→ → → → → → → → → → → → →

*Go on to the next page.*

The starting gun goes off, and the mass of riders surges forward in one tight pack.

You follow behind all day as the caravan of the Tour winds its way toward the north coast and the first-day finish line in the port of Calais.

LaPelle stays back in the pack, and you begin to wonder if he is indeed scared. But as the pack pedals into Calais, it suddenly becomes a two-man race between the two favorites, O'Steen and LaPelle. Both men lean into the last corner as they head for the finish line, side by side, their legs pumping in perfect unison. As the crowd goes wild, another black-jerseyed rider, Oswald Hinckley, comes up fast from behind. O'Steen fades in the last meters, LaPelle wins, and Hinckley nips his teammate O'Steen.

You're at the finish line ready to ask LaPelle for an interview. But he's whisked away by race officials. O'Steen, furious with his young teammate for breaking team policy by beating him, calls the press around him. He accuses LaPelle of pushing him, saying he will file an official protest.

Eddy comes running up, looking pleased with herself. She has overheard LaPelle's manager telling someone to deliver a pair of racing shoes to the Hôtel Jerome. Now all you have to do is find a way in and convince him to give you an interview.

At six o'clock you knock on the door of LaPelle's bungalow in the Hôtel Jerome garden. You're dressed as a messenger and carrying an enormous basket of fruit. Eddy and Jake wait around the corner.

A large blonde woman in a white medical jacket opens the door. You smile and walk right in. The upholstered sofa, kidney-shaped writing table, and ornate mahogany chest reflect the eighteenth-century French rococo style of furniture that fills the room. The woman points you toward a corner already crammed with flowers and baskets of fruit. You hear painful groans from the next room and turn to see LaPelle stretched out on a massage table. A Japanese woman in her bare feet walks along his back.

→ → → → → → → → → → → → →

*Turn to page 69.*

You approach LaPelle. "Mr. LaPelle, this fruit is from America."

He opens one eye and looks you over. "A messenger all the way from America—*ce n'est pas possible*."

"Well, actually, I'm not a messenger, I'm a journalist."

He opens his other eye. "You know I am not giving interviews now. Wait a moment, I think I saw you on *la télévision* when I was in America last year. A person so young, you do very well."

"Thank you. There's just one question I'd like to ask you."

"Okay, if you promise only one." The Eagle groans as a foot works on his neck.

"I understand that someone sabotaged your brakes last week. Is someone trying to hurt you? Or worse?"

LaPelle bolts upright, and the tiny Japanese woman catapults into the air, luckily landing on the bed. LaPelle motions to her and the blonde woman to leave immediately. Then he faces you angrily. "It is absolutely not true! Why would anyone want to hurt me?"

→  →  →  →  →  →  →  →  →  →  →  →  →
*Go on to the next page.*

# 70

There's a sudden crash of glass behind you. An object skitters across the floor under the massage table—sticks of dynamite with a burning fuse. A short fuse! You watch, mesmerized. You can smell the burning cordite. Do you reach under the table, losing valuable seconds, to grab the dynamite and throw it out the window? Or do you run for the door and hope you both get out in time?

→ → → → → → → → → → → → →

*If you decide to throw the bomb,
turn to page 74.*

← ← ← ← ← ← ← ← ← ← ← ← ←

*If you decide to run out of the room,
turn to page 58.*

# 71

Jake smiles when you agree to go along with his plan. You follow him off the roof, and a few minutes later you're running behind him back through the woods. You circle around the boat and come to the animal pens. They are unguarded, as everyone has gone to the monastery for the meeting. You swiftly open all the gates.

Now that you understand Jake's plan, you're into it. You spot the horses, jump up bareback on the stallion, and shout, "Ride'em cowboy!" You motion Jake to get on the mare.

→ → → → → → → → → → → → →
*Go on to the next page.*

Jake, who looks born to ride, gallops with you in front of the charging zoo. Hundreds of animals thunder behind you—elephants, bears, kangaroos, ostriches, armadillos, orangutans, every animal imaginable. This has to be the most bizarre stampede in history.

You hang on to your horse's mane for dear life as you whip through the forest at breakneck speed. You and Jake race into the clearing. The herd of animals behind you tramples the clothesline underfoot and rolls on toward the monastery.

You're swept up in the excitement as you see the monastery looming up ahead. The crowd there has heard the thunder and come out of the cloister to find the animals bearing down on them. The ground shakes as lumbering hippos, wild boars, and trumpeting elephants charge on. Screams, shouts, and animal cries mix in a wild frenzy of movement.

You spot LaPelle wandering about blindfolded. You leap from your horse just in time to lead him behind a tree out of the way of a charging rhinoceros.

The first charge of animals has passed. You yank LaPelle's blindfold off and point to the bicycles leaning against a tree. You jump on one, LaPelle follows suit, and you both career bumpily down the mountain, leaving pandemonium behind you.

← ← ← ← ← ← ← ← ← ← ← ←

*Turn to page 59.*

The fuse burns lower. "Run!" you yell as you dive under the table for the bomb. Marcel LaPelle stumbles out the door. You come up with the dynamite in your trembling right hand and throw it toward the broken window. You duck and cover your head. Nothing happens. You can still hear the *pffft* of the burning fuse. You look up. The dynamite's on the floor by the window. You missed. You lunge and pick it up just as the fuse burns down to the end. Your heart stops. But the dynamite never goes off.

There's a loud crash outside. Even though you have the strength of a wet washcloth, you pull yourself together and run out. Sprawled on the path are Eddy and a young man with a blackened face and clothes. He picks himself up, putting on a black top hat.

"Eddy!" you shout.

"She bolted so fast," Jake explains, "she ran into this man on his bicycle. His ladder came down on her leg."

"I think I broke it," she says with a grimace. The young man in the stovepipe hat keeps rubbing Eddy's leg, repeating a soothing French phrase. Eddy's grimace fades into an appreciative smile.

"Who are you?" you ask the man. "Why were you riding with a ladder?"

The man replies rapidly in French.

"He is a chimney sweep," LaPelle says.

LaPelle turns to you. "What about the bomb?"

"It never went off," you reply. "Monsieur LaPelle, can you call for an ambulance, and also call the police about the bomb?" You watch Eddy with growing concern.

"I will call," LaPelle says, and disappears into the bungalow.

→ → → → → → → → → → → → →

**Turn to page 77.**

"Wait here," you tell Jake and Eddy. You follow LaPelle. You find him examining the bomb.

"You see," he says, as he takes out a stick of dynamite from its plastic wrapping. "They are only wood." A piece of paper falls out. Written in big letters is BOOM! "It is only a prank. I will call the ambulance."

Just then the phone rings. LaPelle picks it up. Although you do not understand what he's saying, the way his body slumps and his voice becomes soft you can tell something strange is going on. He hangs up.

"Who was that?" you ask.

"Just a fan who found out where I was," he answers, and dials a number. He speaks quickly. As he talks, you examine the piece of paper. Something is written in French next to the word BOOM. You can make out the words *femme* and *enfant*.

"The ambulance is coming," LaPelle says.

"And the police?"

"No need for the police. This was only a joke," he says softly. His face is completely white. "We French have a very particular sense of humor, very different from the Anglo-Saxons. Please, don't say anything about this on your program. It is so silly and embarrassing."

→ → → → → → → → → → → →
*Go on to the next page.*

You're sure there's a lot more to the story, but before you can say anything you hear the ambulance outside. Jake insists on going with Eddy, and you agree to drive the van. You and LaPelle wave as they drive off.

"Monsieur LaPelle, if you don't convince me there's a very good reason I shouldn't put it on the air, I'm going to report this incident with the bomb."

Again the color drains from LaPelle's face. He can barely speak. "I will only tell you if you promise not to tell a word to anyone. Not on TV, not to your friends."

"I promise."

LaPelle ushers you into his room. "Two weeks ago I received an anonymous call. I was told that I had better not win the Tour de France, that if I tried, accidents would happen. I've received threats before, so I did not give it any importance. Then I had the problem with the brakes."

You see that the great champion is a very frightened man.

"The writing on the paper with the bomb threatens my wife and child. When I read it I thought I must withdraw from the race. But then the phone rang, and the same voice said I had to stay in the race and help O'Steen win. If I don't, or if I go to the police, my family will pay the price."

"But they can't get away with this!" you blurt.

LaPelle looks at you helplessly.

"There must be something we can do," you say. "Look, I can take your wife and child out of the country and into hiding. You can get police protection and ride to win. Or I can do a thorough investigation and find out who's behind O'Steen. You stay in the race, don't get ahead of O'Steen, and I'll do my best to track down the culprits. What do you think?"

"Both ideas sound good," LaPelle says. "You decide which is better."

→ → → → → → → → → → → → →

**If you decide to hide LaPelle's wife and child, turn to page 111.**

**If you decide to follow O'Steen, turn to page 109.**

A reporter is doing stand-up interviews with tourists passing by the cathedral. She thrusts the microphone in your face. You can see your pursuers running toward you. You're breathing so hard you can't talk. The interviewer smiles, lowers the microphone, and says, "Don't worry, everyone is a little nervous their first time on TV, but there is no reason. You are nice-looking, you will come out well on TV."

She points the microphone toward you again just as the three men run up and join the crowd a few feet away. "So what impresses you most as a tourist about France, or at least about Chartres?"

"Right now," you reply, "I'm most impressed that these three men are trying to kill me."

The interviewer laughs awkwardly. The men don't know what to do. The bystanders gape at them.

You start to tell your story. You relate how LaPelle was threatened and Hinckley murdered. The three men start to back off. Finally they run away.

The journalist rushes you back to her station, and makes you the lead story on French news. The police investigate immediately. The fat doctor confesses that Hinckley was murdered by mistake and Dr. Duchamp killed under instructions from a man whose name he refuses to mention. A day later, a Poli Kako, president of an electronics firm, is arrested. He turns out to be the owner of Team X.

LaPelle, still shaken by the threats, withdraws from the race. Shaun O'Steen goes on to win, as does Team X. But this does not prevent Kako Electronics from avoiding bankruptcy.

You feel you've been pretty lucky. People may criticize television, but you owe your life to it, not to mention your livelihood.

## The End

You look down to see Oswald Hinckley, yesterday's second-place finisher, taking off his black jersey and putting on the yellow.

At the sound of the gun, Hinckley charges out. He builds up a sizable lead in the first five miles, right before a steep climb. You follow behind in the caravan.

"He'll never keep it up," Jake says knowledgeably. "He's young and inexperienced. That yellow jersey has him hyped. He'll crumble soon."

Hinckley pumps up the hill like a demon. He gets to the crest and throws up his fists triumphantly. You watch on the monitor in your vehicle as he crouches low to coast down the other side. Suddenly his bicycle topples over, and he goes sprawling. For a minute he lies twitching on the ground, and then the spasms stop. Hinckley remains motionless. A spectator dashes to his aid. This is no simple fall.

LaPelle, O'Steen, and the others coast by, but they can only glance over, disturbed, and pedal on.

"Grab the camera!" you shout to Jake, as you jump out of the van.

By the time you run up, breathless, a crowd has gathered. The "doo-dwee doo-dwee" of an ambulance parts the onlookers, and you follow right behind.

You see that Hinckley's eyes are wide open, unblinking. Two ambulance attendants run over, check his pulse, and shake their heads. He's dead.

Your mind races. Heart attack? But he was a conditioned athlete. Drugs? Though some riders are known to experiment with drugs, for the race they have to pass drug tests. What about murder? Then it clicks! LaPelle was supposed to be wearing the yellow jersey! And he was warned not to win. Still, there are more than twenty days to go. Killing him at this point would make little sense.

Hinckley's body will be flown to Paris for an autopsy to determine the cause of the rider's premature death. Should you go to Paris to follow up this side of the story and perhaps find another clue about who is behind the threats and possible foul play? Or should you stay and gather more evidence here, keeping your eye on O'Steen?

→ → → → → → → → → → → → →

**If you decide to fly to Paris, turn to page 104.**

← ← ← ← ← ← ← ← ← ← ← ← ←

*If you decide to gather more evidence, turn to page 47.*

You, Jake, and Eddy walk briskly after Kako. He and the trainer cross the street to a park bordering the lake. They step onto a dock and hop into a waiting speedboat. The driver revs the engines, and they pull away into the calm, swan-dotted waters of the little harbor. Once clear of the harbor, the driver guns the engines. The boat rises and speeds out into the lake. You can't follow him now.

You notice some public binoculars for tourists on a chrome stand. You rush over, drop in a Swiss franc, and put your eyes to the lenses. The speedboat is pulling into a little harbor by a distinctive, handsome château. "That shouldn't be hard to identify," you tell Jake and Eddy.

Two hours later you and Eddy are ringing the bell at the gate of the *Château de Daphne*. When you show your press card, the butler answers quickly, "Monsieur Kako does not receive the press, especially without an appointment."

A stick flies over the wall and lands on the ground near you. Loud barking and scratching sounds come from the other side of the wall. You retrieve the stick just as Mr. Kako opens the door. He looks you over, smiles, and holds out his hand for the stick.

"Mr. Kako," you say quickly, "I'm a journalist, and I know that you are the man behind Team X. My partners and I followed you from the bank. Now I want to talk to you about Marcel LaPelle."

A minute later you and Eddy are sitting on Kako's veranda looking over the lake. "You're very enterprising," Kako says. "The press of the world has been after me. Congratulations. I should offer you a job in my company doing public relations." He leans back on his wicker chair and stares across the lake toward the Jura Mountains. "You know only half the story, and if you were to go public with that much, it could be disastrous. I think I can trust you. I will tell you everything if you promise to wait until LaPelle is safe to break it."

You look at Eddy, then say, "That sounds fair."

← ← ← ← ← ← ← ← ← ← ← ← ←

*Turn to page 49.*

Half an hour later a middle-aged woman whom you've gotten out of bed sits watching the monitors. She's deaf, and she's reading lips. She writes down the words. A lab technician who speaks English translates what the woman has written. You find out that the man in the limousine said, "Stop him," and the last words of the man on the phone were, "too late." You pat the editing console and thank the deaf woman for her help.

"Now all we have to find out is who the man in the limousine is," you say excitedly.

"Hold on," Jake interrupts. "You're assuming Hinckley was murdered. We have to wait for the autopsy report for that."

"I'm sure of it."

The lab technician chimes in. "That man in the limousine, everyone in France knows his face. He's Poli Kako, president of the big electronics company. He is also a playboy."

"A playboy? He looks so ugly," Jake says.

"With every million, they say he gets better-looking," the lab technician jokes.

You call up an information network on your computer to get data on Kako. What you find fits the picture you're developing. Kako Electronics has hit bad times—their new generation of equipment is not selling well. Kako himself has been looking for financing. It's rumored that he also has gambling debts. Then you spot a clue

that clinches it: he's been known for his unortho-
dox and imaginative advertising methods.

"He's our man," you confide to Jake.

"But this isn't proof. To nail someone as powerful as that, you have to catch him in the act," Jake
argues.

Jake's got a good point. You need a plan to
expose Kako. You look around the room. It's all
Kako equipment. You spy a miniature, button-
sized camera. You've got it! You reach for the
phone.

"I'm calling Peterson," you tell Jake.

After a few rings, a gruff voice says, "Hello?"

"Boss, it's me. How would you like to broadcast
a live murder confession by one of Europe's
richest men? I want you to stand by ready for it.
It could play to a billion people."

After you hang up, Jake, totally flabbergasted,
says, "What in the world are you planning?
You're crazy."

→ → → → → → → → → → → → →

**Go on to the next page.**

"I'm going to put that minicamera on and go talk to Mr. Kako. I'll be transmitting to you in the van. You satellite uplink the transmission, and the world will have it."

"Now I know you're crazy," says Jake. "If you're right about Kako, you're going to be the first person murdered live on international TV with a billion people watching. If you're wrong, you're going to make a complete fool of yourself in front of the whole world."

You get through to Kako on the phone after telling his underlings you have proof on videotape that he murdered Hinckley. Kako calls your story preposterous, and accuses you of inventing it just to have an interview with him. But he says he admires your initiative. Even though it's after midnight, he invites you to a late dinner. He claims he's an insomniac and gets his best work done at night. You accept his invitation.

You rush back to your hotel to change. When you reach your room, it's been ransacked.

"I told you, Jake," you say. "Kako's our man. He's looking for that tape. Can't you see? He's the one behind Team X—he needs O'Steen to win, so he's the one threatening LaPelle. He killed Hinckley by mistake, and now he's running scared."

"He's scared?" Jake says. "You're the one who should be scared. You really want to walk into the lion's den? This time we have enough evidence that the police might listen."

As you fix the minicamera onto your shirt, someone bangs on the door.

Jake walks toward the knocking, "Who's there?"

"The police!"

# 90

"One moment," you shout, "I'm not dressed."
You whisper to Jake, "Kako! He's called the police. Who are they going to believe?"

The pounding grows louder. You glance toward the open window. You're on the second floor. You've got a choice. You can either go out the window and with luck keep your rendezvous with Mr. Kako and a worldwide television audience. Or you can avoid the risk, open the door, and explain everything to the police.

An ax smashes through a panel of the door.

← ← ← ← ← ← ← ← ← ← ← ← ←

*If you decide to jump out the window,*
*turn to page 23.*

→ → → → → → → → → → → → →

*If you decide to open the door,*
*turn to page 101.*

You hold your arms high above your head, waving your press card hopefully. The bearded, grim-faced men thunder down the slope toward you.

One of them approaches you. Looking into his eyes, you get the sinking feeling he's capable of anything. His hand flicks out and grabs your card. He smiles as he studies it. "Radio, television, or newspaper?"

For some reason you feel your life depends on the answer. "Well," he demands again, "Which? Or maybe you are not any of them, but a cop."

You gulp. "No, no, television. I'm a television reporter."

They all look at each other. "Television!"

You try to think fast. "Yes, television. I could get your message through to the world. Millions would hear and see it. Of course, only if you wanted."

"The world is too stupid to listen to our message. We have tried. We don't need messages, we need money!" shouts the leader.

"Television is a very bad influence, especially on children," an older man opines.

→ → → → → → → → → → → → →

**Go on to the next page.**

"Well, in general I agree," you stammer. "We think we make quality programs. But I agree there is much too much violence. On my program we are very much against violence. I personally am very much against violence." You rattle on. "I hope that you share with me the value of nonviolence, both on television and in real life."

"You are going to make the porters very happy," the leader interrupts.

Well, you think, that's a positive statement. You force a smile.

"The porters are the ones who have to carry the bird food every day all the way up this mountain. You are, so to speak, last on the pecking order. Today you are bird food."

Those two silly words, "bird food," are the last ones you ever hear.

## The End

You are taken into a large dining room with a very long table. Mr. Kako sits at the far end, eating. There's enough light from the crystal chandeliers to transmit a clear picture. You pray that Jake is picking this up.

Kako looks up, hiding his surprise. "My apologies for beginning without you. I thought you must have been detained." The intensity of his one eye is more than most men can muster in two.

You put the videotape on the table and slide it all the way to his end. "You didn't have to mess up my room looking for this."

He takes the tape and throws it in the fireplace.

You shake your head, "Burning plastic is very bad for the ecosystem."

"I, too, am interested in methods of disposal. I've thought a great deal of how to dispose of you. If you prefer preserving the balance of nature, I could feed you to my shark," Kako says matter-of-factly.

"Are you threatening me?" You make sure the camera is pointed right at him.

→ → → → → → → → → → → → →

**Go on to the next page.**

"Certainly not. To threaten you would be a sign of weakness. I'm telling you what I'm going to do. I've worked too hard on this plan to see some miserable television reporter destroy my life's work. Killing Hinckley was a stupid error. Killing you will be an intelligent pleasure." Kako motions to his bodyguard to take you away. "Oh," he adds, "and you won't be needing the usual guest towel. There won't be anything left to dry off."

"Hold on!" you interject. "Turn on your television right now and I think you will change your mind."

He frowns. "As the condemned's last wish, all right."

He turns on the large-screen Kako-brand set behind him. On screen is the back of a man in front of a television. Kako turns and shrugs. You walk quickly around him toward the set. He turns to follow you, then catches sight of the man on TV turning as well. Kako can't believe the mirror image he sees. He moves an arm, he makes a face. It's him.

→ → → → → → → → → → → →

*Go on to the next page.*

"The whole world is watching this right now, Kako," you say, as he stands in a state of shock. "I would like to interrupt this interview for a commercial message. I personally can testify to the quality of Kako products. These images could not be brought to you if it were not for this astounding Kako camera."

Kako knocks you down as he bolts toward the door. You hit your head on the table, momentarily stunned. Then you head after Kako and bump into Jake on his way in to get you.

You hear the squeal of tires and run to the window to see a Rolls-Royce peel out of the driveway.

You and Jake rush to follow in the van. You take the wheel. "Hold tight!" you call.

Jake looks over his shoulder. The speedometer of the van appears on the TV monitor—your camera's still on. Grabbing his own camera, Jake switches the signal to it, so the world is now getting a real chase.

Kako pays no regard to stop signs or lights, racing right through them. You tear through the narrow streets, drawing closer. As you flash by a shop full of TV sets in the window, you see your own image streak by.

You're right behind Kako now. Suddenly the Rolls skids out on a ninety-degree corner. You deliberately smash into it. This is better than bumper cars! Jake, safely strapped in his seat belt, is still filming away.

You both hop out. The Roll's electrical system is out. All the doors are automatically locked. Kako pounds on the windows. He's a prisoner among his gadgets, none of which will work without electrical power.

Sirens sound and in moments the police are there. A tow truck hauls the Rolls off to the police station with the imprisoned Kako inside. The police tell you they saw it all on TV, as did much of the world. As they say this, Jake continues to film, so they too are now being viewed by the world on TV.

The French government, deeply grateful that you have saved the Tour de France, awards you and Jake the *Legion d'Honneur*. You are the toast of France.

## The End

"**H**old your horses," you tell the police, who are smashing in the door. You unlatch the locks, and five police officers rush in. Two grab you, whirl you around, and latch handcuffs on your wrists. Jake, too, gets cuffed. You are hustled off to the police station.

At the station, you and Jake are shoved into a little white room, followed by a dozen police and the captain of the department. The captain speaks English. "We have a problem here, no?" he says.

"Yes, a big problem. There is a problem of murder on the Tour de France—"

He cuts you right off. "You are in serious trouble. I don't want to hear any fanciful nonsense. We were informed that you tried to blackmail Mr. Poli Kako with this tape." He holds up a videocassette.

You leap up. "No! Of course not. We are journalists."

The captain refuses to listen, and you and Jake are thrown in jail. Two hours later, a representative from the American consulate arrives. He is able to free you on bail. He tells you he was helped by the fact that the tape turned out to be children's cartoons. You will see a judge in the morning.

You're really steamed by the time you get back to the hotel. "It's unjust," Jake agrees, "but this Kako is obviously a very powerful man."

→ → → → → → → → → → → → →

*Go on to the next page.*

"I may be late," you retort, "but I'm going to keep my rendezvous with him. If I go now, in the middle of the night, I'll catch him off guard."

Ten minutes later, you arrive at Kako's walled-in estate. You look through the grill in the gate and see a light on in a downstairs room. You hesitate, your finger on the bell. Deciding to make your visit a complete surprise, you pull yourself up the ivy-covered wall and drop into the garden.

You sneak stealthily through the darkness. You hear something behind you and look back to see bared white teeth. By the light from the house you can glimpse a massive Doberman.

You sprint toward the house. There's another wall, but it's low. You leap up, grab the top, and pull yourself up. The dog barks below you, thrashing at the wall.

The top of the wall is narrow. Suddenly flood-lights come on. You lose your balance but manage to direct your fall away from the dog's side.

*Splash!* You've fallen into a swimming pool. How lucky, you think. Then you feel something brush by you underwater. A fin breaks the surface, and a massive shark twists out of the water toward you. There's a tingling sensation in what used to be your leg. You realize you've just covered your last story.

**The End**

You catch the next flight to Paris. Once there, you speak with Dr. Duchamp, one of the coroners who has just finished examining Hinckley's body. "We found poison in his system," he tells you. "And a tiny puncture mark on his neck."

"Poison? What kind of poison?"

"One so new to our Western knowledge there is no scientific name. The Amazonian Indians call it *malakas*. The smallest trace will kill you instantly."

"And the mark on his neck—how did he get that?" you ask.

"My guess is from a needle shot from some kind of air-pressure gun—the same principle as an Amazonian blowgun."

"So your conclusion is murder," you prompt.

Dr. Duchamp looks absently at a paper on his desk. "Come back in two hours. I'm giving a press conference and will hand out the final report."

You thank him and leave. Murder on the Tour de France! This is a major story. The two hours go slowly. You sit at a little sidewalk bistro drinking *café au lait*, thick expresso coffee mixed with steaming milk. It's as good as ice cream.

At the press conference, you notice a plaque indicating that the new wing of the hospital was donated by Poli Kako. A fat man in a white lab coat appears at a small door and strides to the lectern. Flashbulbs spark and cameras whir. It's not Dr. Duchamp.

"We have examined Oswald Hinckley's body," the fat doctor says, "and concluded that the cause of death was a heart attack."

Shouts from the press resound in the room. "What caused the heart attack?"

The doctor lifts a hand for silence. "No drugs, but overexertion. He had a weak aortic valve, a genetic flaw. He would not have survived long in any case."

After the press conference, you return to Duchamp's office. He's not there. Instead, the doctor who gave the press conference is clearing the papers from Duchamp's desk.

"Where's Dr. Duchamp?" you ask.

"Are you the reporter he spoke to earlier?" the man asks, as he puts papers in a box. A fold of fat hangs over his collar.

"Yes. He told me Hinckley had been murdered with poison."

The doctor laughs. "Poor Duchamp. He was taken away to a mental institution this afternoon. Since his research trip to the Amazon last year, he hasn't been the same. He diagnosed every corpse that came in here, whether it was cancer or an auto accident, as death by *malakas* poisoning."

"There's no mark on Hinckley's neck?"

→ → → → → → → → → → → → →

*Go on to the next page.*

"Perhaps a mosquito bite. There was no poison, I can assure you. You are welcome to look at the body. Though perhaps you are squeamish about these things."

"No," you lie. "I'm a professional, I'm used to it."

The doctor looks nervous to you. Something strange is definitely going on.

You change your mind about viewing the body. "But I have no time at present," you blurt to the fat doctor. "I'm late for an appointment."

You rush from the room, down the stairs, and into the streets of the Left Bank, heading toward the River Seine. Looking back, you see two men in sunglasses and white medical coats running, too. A bus stops nearby, and you dash on board. From the window you see the men pop into a car and follow.

On the outskirts of Paris, the bus reaches the end of the line. The driver whistles for you to leave. Across the street is a small airport filled with private planes. The men following you leave their car and pretend to be window shopping in front of a boutique. You walk into the airport as if you purposely came here.

You approach a young man behind the information counter, and say, "I want to hire a pilot right now."

The young man pulls out a pilot's hat from under the counter. "My name is Francois, your pilot."

You hear the door behind you click shut. The two white-coated men smile at you but say nothing.

The young pilot grabs your arm, pulls you through a door, locks it with a metal rod, and runs out on the tarmac toward a small plane.

In no time you're in the air. You see your pursuers scampering around like ants trapped in a glass jar.

"Where to?" the young man says with a self-satisfied smile.

"I'm a tourist," you say. "I don't know France well. Show me the sights."

"Then we must go to Chartres," he bubbles. "There is a most magnificent cathedral there. No one has lived until they've been in this cathedral."

You try to relax and enjoy the view of the countryside, as you fly toward Chartres. You can see why France has produced such incredible artists as Matisse, Monet, Renoir, and Toulouse-Lautrec.

→ → → → → → → → → → → → →

*Go on to the next page.*

# 108

Chartres lies only forty-five minutes southwest of Paris by plane. Soon the twin towers of the great cathedral rise like ship masts from the seemingly endless sea of wheat and corn. When you land at a nearby airport, the young man reaches under his seat and pulls out a chauffeur's cap. "I can use my cousin's limo service to take you to the cathedral," he offers.

Minutes later you stand inside the nave of the awesome cathedral where everything seems to soar heavenward. Brilliant panels of enormous stained glass illuminate the interior. Your pilot, now wearing a hat that says GUIDE, explains that the cathedral, a perfect example of Gothic architecture, was built in the thirteenth century.

You'd be more awestruck if you weren't worried that three men in navy jackets didn't seem to be closing in on you. You quickly move outside, and the three men follow.

← ← ← ← ← ← ← ← ← ← ← ←

*Turn to page 80.*

That night, after you have visited Eddy at the hospital and found out she has to be in traction for three weeks, you edit the day's footage and write your commentary.

"You're not even going to mention the fake bomb?" Jake asks, surprised.

"No. I want to concentrate on O'Steen, go after the Team X angle and find out who's behind it." You can't tell Jake what LaPelle told you.

The next morning you keep your eye on O'Steen as he does his warm-ups and approaches the starting line next to LaPelle. LaPelle smiles. O'Steen frowns, regarding LaPelle's yellow jersey with envy.

The starting gun is raised. The official clock shows fifteen seconds to go. Fourteen ... thirteen ... But an official runs in, blowing a whistle, and the clock stops. The riders grumble. The official walks up to LaPelle, says something, and removes The Eagle's yellow jersey. "What's going on?" you exclaim.

A Japanese journalist next to you answers, "A one-minute penalty. They allowed O'Steen's protest from yesterday's race." He holds out his portable TV. On screen is a replay of yesterday's incident—LaPelle leaning over to O'Steen and shoving him. O'Steen wobbles and hits the edge of the gravel, and LaPelle moves ahead.

"That was just a nudge," Jake retorts.

← ← ← ← ← ← ← ← ← ← ← ←

*Turn to page 82.*

You fly to the city of Marseilles on the south coast of France, where LaPelle's wife Angelique and their baby Sasha live. Marseille, France's oldest and second-largest city, was founded in 600 B.C. by Greek adventurers. Its rocky shoreline is broken by many inlets. Perhaps wrongly so, the city is also known for its many gangsters.

You find LaPelle's quaint tile-roofed house at the end of a winding road just outside the city. It sits on a beautiful hill overlooking the green Mediterranean Sea. You knock on the thick wooden door, and Angelique answers. A tall, pleasant-looking woman with blonde hair, she holds her six-month-old baby in her arms.

You introduce yourself.

"Yes," she says with a worried look, pulling you quickly inside. "Marcel called last night and told me you were coming. There has been a man watching this house these last days. He seems familiar to me, but I have not been able to get a close look at him."

She pulls back the curtain slightly and peeks out the window. "He's there, sitting in that black car."

You lead Angelique with the baby out the back door, carrying their suitcases. You load up her Volvo sedan and drive out onto the main street. The black car follows you. You speed up. So does your pursuer. You screech around a traffic circle surrounded by crumbling, two-story houses, but the man keeps up with you.

"Hold on!" you shout as you dart the wrong way down a gritty, narrow, one-way street. When cars approach you head on, you zip down a side street. This time your follower misjudges and slams into a telephone pole. He backs up and gradually catches up until you're side by side. You can see his stubbly face clearly.

"Oh, no!" Angelique cries. "It's Robert!"

Robert waves a pistol, motioning you to pull over. The crazy look in his eye doesn't give you much choice.

You jam the accelerator to the floor and pull into a curvy stretch just above the sea, headed for Monaco, a paradise retreat of the rich and famous almost entirely taken up by the city of Monte Carlo. If you get there alive, LaPelle's manager has a motor launch waiting to take you to Italy.

"Robert was my first love, and a very good friend of Marcel's," Angelique explains. "He was a great rider. He even used to beat Marcel. But six years ago he came very fast into a tunnel. So did a car from the other end. He was never the same afterward. He became very bitter, and a bit *fou*, crazy. Then I married Marcel. Robert was a good man, but he became involved with bad people here in Marseilles."

You see no sign of Robert in the rearview mirror, but the road is so full of curves, he might be only a short way behind.

You cross into Monaco and head for the port. The motor launch is waiting. The captain guns the engines, and you head for open water. Angelique shouts and points back to the dock. You see Robert limping up a gangplank and onto a motor launch of the same type you're in.

You choose a new destination and order the captain to head west. "Where to?" he says.

"Arles," you reply, indicating a city on the Rhône River a short distance inland.

The chase goes on. You stay just out of range of the gun you know Robert is carrying. Under normal circumstances, nothing could be more agreeable than being on a private boat in the Mediterranean, but this is a tense nightmare.

As you approach Arles, you are taken even in your anxiety with its beauty—olive trees, grape vines, and Roman architecture. This area, in fact, was once part of the Roman Empire. In Arles, a picturesque city, the Dutch painter Vincent van Gogh did some of his best work.

→ → → → → → → → → → → → →

*Go on to the next page.*

You see a train station near the river and tell the captain to pull to shore. As you and Angelique run with the baby up the riverbank, Robert's boat comes into view. You reach the station. A conductor waves you aboard the train and closes the doors. You've outrun Robert at last!

The train moves out. Through the window in your compartment, you see Robert hobble up the riverbank and into a taxi. "No need to worry," says Angelique. "These modern French trains move much faster than a car."

A few minutes later a conductor slides open the door to your compartment. *Billets?* he says. "Tickets?" You reach for your wallet. A sinking feeling overcomes you. No wallet. You last had it in the boat—did you drop it in your haste?

Angelique doesn't have any money, either. She appeals to the conductor with a rapid-fire explanation, tears, and pleadings. He nods, says something calmly to her, and leaves.

"Looks like you did a good job," you say.

"No. We have to get off at the next station."

The next station is a small hut with a waiting room, ticket booth, and timetable. You step outside. You're farther inland, and the countryside is a maze of arid, scrub-covered hills. A taxi driver leans against his beat-up Renault. With a stubbly beard, an expired cigarette stuck to his lip, and wearing the popular French beret, he sizes you up and asks in English, "Want a taxi?"

"Yes, but we have no money," you tell the taxi driver.

"I only drive for money," he says. "Perhaps you have a credit card?"

Why yes, you think suddenly—you always keep one in your shoe when you travel in case your pocket is picked. You pull it out. He opens the door, ushers you in, and runs the card—thwack—through his machine.

Just then a taxi speeds past you in a billow of dust. Robert is in the back. "Hurry!" you tell the driver.

"The man in the other taxi is chasing us, and he has a gun!" Angelique explains in French. The driver snaps to, steps on the accelerator, and races by the other taxi, which has just turned around. The first taxi spins again and follows.

Hours later you're still bouncing around in the taxi, having been on a Tour de France all your own. Sasha seems to be doing the best, as she sleeps very well in a kind of papoose. You are hot, sore, exhausted, and filthy. You have driven north through the center of France known as the *Massif Central*, the country's stony heart, geographically speaking. The dry hills and mountains of the *Massif* are old, but a huge uplifting of the Alps a few million years ago tilted and cracked the old granite, and volcanoes spewed lava. The land is beautiful, but bleak and unprosperous.

→ → → → → → → → → → → → →

*Turn to page 117.*

The taxis have kept up with each other. Each time Robert's car stops to get gas, you stop at the next station yourselves to fill up.

You don't know what Angelique is thinking, but you are wondering what in the world you are doing in this endless car ride. Several car lengths back is a lunatic murderer who has followed you across land and sea and won't rest until he's cut your throats. You vounteered to help with the most noble of intentions. Saving lives is more important than your journalistic career, but you're almost ready to give up.

That night you reach the city of Le Mans, known for its car races. Your driver suddenly shrieks. The taxi is blocked by an overturned truck. Robert's taxi has pulled alongside you, and Robert is pointing his gun at your driver.

"Go on the sidewalk, and down that alley!" you shout. The driver does so, smashing through a wooden barricade and skidding out onto the Le Mans racetrack. You're right in the middle of a race for ancient automobiles! Robert's taxi is right behind you.

For the next three hours you go around and around, keeping ahead of not only the other taxi but most of the competing cars. Just after the stroke of midnight, however, your driver pulls off the course.

→  →  →  →  →  →  →  →  →  →  →  →  →

*Go on to next page.*

"What are you doing?" you squeak, too exhausted to complain much.

"More money," he says.

"You have my credit card."

He points to the date and says, "Expired." He indicates his digital calendar watch. You've lost all track of time.

The driver forces you all out. You can't believe he's doing this. Surely it's just a bargaining tactic.

A door slams, and you look back. Robert runs from his taxi, waving his pistol high over his head. He fires twice. The noise gets you going. You push Angelique and the baby toward a car repair bay ahead.

Too late! Robert cuts you off. He hobbles over to you shouting. "You abominable kidnapper. Die!"

"No! Don't, Robert! Please!" Angelique screams.

"But this vile man has kidnapped you and led you and your poor baby through every kind of danger. Only a heartless criminal would do that." Robert glares at you as he speaks. "You know I wouldn't let anything happen to you, Angelique. That's why I'm there always looking out for you when Marcel is away. And what luck I was there!"

"But Robert!" you explain. "I thought you were the kidnapper. I was protecting Angelique from you!"

By the time you and Robert get it all straightened out, you are great friends. However, Jake and Eddy have not been able to cover for you at the Tour de France. Mr. Peterson at WCYA is not pleased. You don't dare tell him where you've been in case he fires you for absence of brains rather than just absence from the job.

All in all, you have to admit there's not much to show for your ride. Plus, with the meter on, it had to be the most expensive taxi ride in French history.

## The End

## ABOUT THE AUTHOR

**JAMES BECKET**, a graduate of Williams College and Harvard Law School, has had a varied career as a human rights lawyer, journalist, United Nations official, and filmmaker. He recently wrote and directed the movie *Ulterior Motives*, a thriller. He lived for many years in the French-speaking part of Switzerland where he avidly followed the Tour de France.

## ABOUT THE ILLUSTRATOR

**HOWARD SIMPSON** was born in Newark, New Jersey. He began his professional career drawing storyboards for Action News and Accu-Weather. He soon began illustrating comic books, working for DC Comics and other companies. He now owns a comic-book store in Pennsylvania. Howard also does graphic design, toy design, and computer graphics. He and his wife Stacie live in Maplewood, New Jersey, where they are busy raising their daughters Kira and Melody.